Miffy and the Butterfly

D1517759

Based on the work of **Dick Bruna**
Story written by **R. J. Cregg**

SIMON SPOTLIGHT

New York   London   Toronto   Sydney   New Delhi

SIMON SPOTLIGHT
An imprint of Simon & Schuster Children's Publishing Division
1230 Avenue of the Americas, New York, New York 10020
This Simon Spotlight paperback edition May 2018
Published in 2018 by Simon & Schuster, Inc. Publication licensed by Mercis Publishing bv, Amsterdam.
Stories and images are based on the work of Dick Bruna.
'Miffy and Friends' © copyright Mercis Media bv, all rights reserved.
All rights reserved, including the right of reproduction in whole or in part in any form.
SIMON SPOTLIGHT and colophon are registered trademarks of Simon & Schuster, Inc.
For information about special discounts for bulk purchases, please contact Simon & Schuster Special Sales
at 1-866-506-1949 or business@simonandschuster.com.
Manufactured in the United States of America 0318 LAK
10 9 8 7 6 5 4 3 2 1
ISBN 978-1-5344-1115-9
ISBN 978-1-5344-1116-6 (eBook)

It is a beautiful spring day. Miffy is playing in her yard at home. "Look at these beautiful flowers!" Miffy says.

Miffy leans in to the red petals. "These flowers smell like spring!" she says.
Uh-oh, Miffy's nose tickles.

Ah . . . ahh . . . achoo! Miffy sneezes.
Suddenly a bright yellow butterfly flies out of the bush.
"Hello!" Miffy says to the butterfly. "Your wings look
ust like flower petals," she says.

The butterfly flits right above Miffy's head. She reaches out to touch it, but the butterfly flies away.

"Come back here!" Miffy calls. She would like to touch the butterfly's soft wings. She waves her arms and leaps to catch it.

Daddy sees Miffy leaping around the yard. He stops pulling carrots for a moment. "I wish I had your energy, Miffy," he calls. "Digging is hard work."

Miffy decides that leaping after butterflies is hard work too. She stops for a moment to rest and say hello to Snuffy.

"Hello, Snuffy!" Miffy says. "I'm trying to catch this butterfly. Will you help me?"

Miffy doesn't see that her friend Melanie has run into her yard.

Miffy turns to run after her butterfly and bumps into Melanie.

"Oh hi, Miffy!" Melanie says. "I'm sorry I ran into you. I was chasing a butterfly."

"That's okay," Miffy says. "I was chasing a butterfly too!"
Snuffy barks. The butterflies are flying away!

Both butterflies land on a bush and rest their wings.

"Miffy, look!" Melanie says. "The butterflies are over there."

"Let's be very quiet and sneak up on them," Miffy says.

Snuffy stays behind.

The two friends walk as quietly as can be on the tips of their toes.

"We're almost there," Miffy whispers to Melanie.

With just a few steps left, Miffy holds her breath. She leans forward to touch the butterflies and steps on a tiny twig.

Snap! The twig makes a sound and scares the butterflies away!

"Don't lose them!" Melanie says.

Miffy and Melanie chase the butterflies all the way to Daddy's ears!

"Oh, Daddy fell asleep in his chair!" Miffy whispers to Melanie with a giggle.

"We better not wake him up," Melanie says. The two girls move in close to the butterflies.

The yellow butterfly flies from Daddy's ear to his nose.

Ah . . . ahh . . . achoo! Daddy wakes himself up with a sneeze.

"Daddy," Miffy says, "you've scared off my butterfly. I almost caught it!"

"I'm sorry, Miffy, but you shouldn't try to catch butterflies. You could hurt them. Your butterfly is probably back where you first found it."

Miffy shows Daddy and Melanie where she first found the butterfly.
"It was on the bush with red flowers," Miffy says.

"Butterflies do like flowers," Daddy says. But there are no butterflies to be seen.

"How exactly did you find the butterfly, Miffy?" Melanie asks.

"I was smelling a flower like this," Miffy says, leaning in to the sweet smelling petals. Daddy and Melanie bend down to smell the flowers too. "And I was very quiet because you need to be quiet to see a butterfly." This time, everyone's noses begin to tickle!

Ah . . . ahh . . . achoo! Miffy, Daddy, and Melanie all sneeze at once. Suddenly dozens of butterflies flutter out of the bush!

"I thought you said we had to be very quiet," Melanie says to Miffy.

"Sometimes being very noisy can work too!" Miffy says.

"Aren't the butterflies beautiful?" Daddy asks.
"Like flying flowers!" Miffy says.
"Just like flying flowers," Daddy agrees.
"Hooray for butterflies!" Miffy and Melanie cheer.